W9-CFV-297

The Mud Flat Olympics

by James Stevenson

Greenwillow Books
~ NEW YORK ~

Watercolor paints and a black pen were used for the
full-color art. The text type is Leawood Book.
Printed in Singapore by Tien Wah Press

First Edition   10 9 8 7 6 5 4 3 2

Library of Congress Cataloging-in-Publication Data
Stevenson, James (date)
The Mud Flat Olympics / by James Stevenson.
p.   cm.
Summary: At the Mud Flat Olympics if the
animals don't win the Deepest Hole Contest,
the All-Snail High Hurdles, or the River-Cross
Freestyle, they can still come to the picnic after
the games and have ice cream for dessert.
ISBN 0-688-12923-4 (trade).
ISBN 0-688-12924-2 (lib. bdg.)
[1. Animals—Fiction.   2. Games—Fiction.]
I. Title.   PZ7.S84748Mu   1994   [E]—dc20
93-28118   CIP   AC

MORNING

"I hear something," said Ardsley.

"Something in the woods," said Hastings.

"Somebody's running," said Ardsley.

"The earth is shaking," said Sidney.
"Maybe it's Burbank!" said Stanley.
"Is today the big day?" said Sammy.

Then Burbank ran out of the woods
carrying his torch.

"Let the Olympic games begin!" yelled
Burbank, and everybody cheered.

8

1

THE DEEPEST HOLE CONTEST

"The Deepest Hole Contest is about to begin," said Harold, the judge.

"Are you ready, Kevin?"

"Ready, Harold!" said Kevin.

"Are you ready, Kimberly?" said Harold.

"Raring to go!" said Kimberly.

"And you, Mr. Crenshaw?"

"What?" said old Mr. Crenshaw. "Speak up!"

"Are you ready to dig?" yelled Harold.
"I've done it every year since 1902,"
 said Mr. Crenshaw. "Let's go!"
"On your marks. . .get set. . .dig!" said
 Harold.
The dirt flew in the air. When Harold
opened his eyes, Kevin and Kimberly
were out of sight. . . .

But Mr. Crenshaw hadn't gone very far.
"How are you doing, Mr. Crenshaw?"
called Harold.

"Don't bother me!" said Mr. Crenshaw.
"I'm trying to win the Olympics."
"Aren't you a little tired?" asked Harold.
"I'm pacing myself," said Mr. Crenshaw.
"I save my best digging for the end."

Harold put his ear to the ground.

"Who's ahead?" asked Clarence.

"Hard to tell," said Harold. "But they're
both way down there."

"Sounds to me like Kimberly might be
a few yards deeper," said Clarence.

"Not by much," said Harold. "This is very
exciting."

Soon everybody was listening.

"Kevin's ahead," said Doris.

"No, that's Kimberly," said Vince.

"How can you tell?" asked Linn.

"They have different styles," said Doris.

"But which one is which?" said Linn.

"Good point," said Harold.

"I'm dropping out," said Mr. Crenshaw.

"I'm pooped."

"That's very sensible, Mr. Crenshaw," said
  Harold.

"I gave it my best shot," said Mr. Crenshaw.

"You can't ask for more than that."

The sounds of digging got fainter and fainter.
After a while everybody stopped listening.
"They must be really far down," said Vince.
"I hope they're all right," said Doris.

Suddenly Kevin appeared.
Everybody clapped.

Then Kimberly burst out of the ground.

Everybody cheered.

"So, Harold, who won?" said Vince.

"Well," said Harold, "I'm not exactly sure yet."

"You're the judge, Harold!" said Doris.

"I know," said Harold. "Just be patient."

He turned to Kevin. "Could you tell me,
Kevin, how deep you dug?"

"Well," said Kevin, "I dug for what must have
been several hundred miles through solid
rock. Very tough. But I kept going."
"And then?" said Harold.
"Hot lava," said Kevin. "I was at the center
of the earth. That's when I turned back."

The crowd clapped.

"Strong," said Vince. "Kevin's strong."

"Brave," said Doris. "Very brave."

"Good distance," said Mr. Crenshaw.

Harold turned to Kimberly.

"How deep did you go, Kimberly?
Did you get to hot lava, too?"

"Went right through it, Harold,"
said Kimberly.

"Wasn't it awfully warm?" said Harold.

"Yes, but I was moving fast," said Kimberly.

"What did you come to next?" asked
Harold.

"Rock, then dirt."

"And?"

"Then I suddenly came out into sunlight!"

"Where were you?" said Harold.

"I don't know," said Kimberly, "but everybody was speaking Chinese!"

"Kimberly wins!" yelled Vince. The crowd cheered. "Hooray for Kimberly!"

"You're the winner, Kimberly," said Harold, and handed her the medal for Deepest Hole.

"Too bad, Kevin," said Vince. "I thought you were going to win."

"Maybe next year," said Kevin. "I'm going to practice every day till then."

"Speed-digging?" said Vince. "Dirt and rock?"

"No," said Kevin. "Making up stories."

THE ALL-SNAIL
HIGH HURDLES

"Everybody ready for the All-Snail High Hurdle event?" said Burbank.

"Yes."

"Yes."

"Yes."

"Yes."

"Yes."

"On your marks. . . get set . . . go!" said Burbank.

The snails moved ahead.

"Please hurry," said Burbank. "I have a lunch date."

Half an hour later they were approaching
the first hurdle.

"That hurdle looks high," said Sidney.

"And steep," said Sally.

"This won't be easy," said Sammy.

"Could you all stop talking about it and
just do it?" asked Burbank.

Stanley started up the hurdle.

"You really need to be strong and know
what you're doing," said Stanley. "I'll
show you how."

The others watched.

"Look at him go," said Sonya.

"Hold on tight, Stan," called Sammy.

"I am almost to the top," said Stanley.
"Only a little further and . . . oh-oh . . .

"Ohh . . ."

Stanley came sliding down backward.

"That's slippery," said Stanley.

"You're slippery," said Sally.

"We're all slippery," said Sammy.

"Never mind who's slippery!" said
Burbank. "This is supposed to be
a race! Hurry up!"

"Who's next?" asked Sidney.

"Not me."

"Not me."

"Me, either."

"Somebody!" said Burbank. "Please!"

"Well," said Sidney, "I'll give it a whirl."

Sidney slithered slowly up the hurdle.

"Now we're getting somewhere," said
Burbank.
Finally Sidney reached the top.

"Good going, Sid!"
cried Sonya.
"Nice climb!"
called Sammy.
"How's the view, Sid?"
called Sally.

"I don't know," said Sidney. "I get dizzy
 if I look down."

"Keep moving, Sid," called Burbank.
"I'm already late for lunch."
"Okay," said Sidney. "I'll try. . . ."
 Suddenly Sidney vanished.
 Then there was a thunk!

"Sidney?" called Sammy.

"Sidney?" called Sally.

There was no answer.

Sally and Sammy peered around the
side of the hurdle.

"Are you all right, Sid?" asked Sally.

"I guess so," said Sidney. "Coming
down was a lot faster than going up."

"I'm leaving for lunch," said Burbank.
"I'll be back long before anybody wins,
that much I know!"
He left.

"Burbank is trying to hint that we're
slow," said Stanley.
"We are extremely swift snails," said Sonya.
"And smarter than Burbank, too," said
Sidney.
"Why don't we show him how smart
we are?" said Stanley.

When Burbank got back from lunch, all
the snails were sitting on the finish line.
"What?" cried Burbank. "You finished?"
"Hours ago," said Sammy.
"Those hurdles aren't hard once you get
the hang of it," said Sally.
"Up and over," said Sidney. "No problem."

"I just can't believe it," said Burbank.

"Who won?"

"You're the judge," said Sonya.

"But I missed the finish," said Burbank.

"I was having lunch."

"Now who's slow?" said Sidney.

"We all won," said Stanley. "All of us
 snails."

3

MR. TOKAY
WINS AGAIN

"I don't like this part of the Olympics,"
said Mrs. Collard. "I don't want to be
a judge."
"I don't, either," said Mr. Filbert, "but
somebody has to do it."
"I hope there aren't too many contestants,"
said Mrs. Collard.
"Well, let's get it over with," said
Mr. Filbert.
They sat down at the judges' table.

"Have you got your score cards?"
said Mrs. Collard.

"All set," said Mr. Filbert.

Mr. Sorrell finished putting up the big sign
behind them:

"Bring in the first contestant,"
said Mrs. Collard.

Gordon was first.

"Go ahead, Gordon," said Mrs. Collard.

"Oh, my goodness," said Mr. Filbert,
rubbing his eyes.

They voted with their score cards.

"Next!" said Mrs. Collard.

Burnet came next.

"Good heavens!" said Mrs. Collard.

"Maybe we should take a break?" said
Mr. Filbert.

They gave Burnet an eight and a seven.

"How many more?" said Mrs. Collard.

"I don't know," said Mr. Filbert. "This is
difficult."

Franklin was next. He was very young.

"Go ahead, Franklin," said Mrs. Collard.

"Do the best you can."

"I already did," said Franklin.

"Oh," said Mrs. Collard. "Of course."

They both gave him a five.

Old Mr. Tokay was next.

"Didn't you win last year?" asked Mr. Filbert.
"And the year before that," said
 Mr. Tokay. "Ready when you are!"
"Any time," said Mr. Filbert.
"Brace yourself," whispered Mrs. Collard
 to Mr. Filbert.

Mrs. Collard and Mr. Filbert shrieked.

The score cards went flying.

"Well?" said Mr. Tokay. "How did I do?"

There was no answer.

Mr. Sorrell came by.

"Congratulations, Mr. Tokay," he said.

"Looks like you're still champion."

"Thank you," said Mr. Tokay, and he
went home.

THE RIVER-CROSS
FREESTYLE

Ardsley and Hastings were heading for the river when they saw Waldorf looking sad.

"What's the matter, Waldy?" said Hastings.

"I wish the Olympics were over," said Waldorf. "I never win anything."

"How about the River-cross Freestyle?" said Ardsley. "Why don't you enter that? You're a good swimmer."

"We're going to do it," said Hastings. "Come
on along."

"Well," said Waldorf. "I'll keep you company,
but I don't know about the race."

They came to the river bank.

"Want to get in the race?"
said May. "I'm the judge."

"Yes, please," said Ardsley.

"Absolutely," said Hastings.

"Who else is in it?" said Waldorf.

"Hugh," said May.

Hugh was warming up, doing jumping jacks
and push-ups.

"Well," said Waldorf, "maybe you could
put me down for the race."

They lined up on the starting line.

"I'd say your chances are pretty good,
Waldy," said Ardsley.

"There are only four of us," said Hastings.

"I could come in fourth. That's what will
happen," said Waldorf.

"Ready. . .set. . .swim!" said May.

They all went into the water and started
for the far side of the river.

"Look at Waldorf!" said Hastings. "He's
 cooking!"
"Way to go, Waldy!" called Ardsley.

Waldorf was in the lead when suddenly
there was a big splash back at the starting
line.
It was Crocker the crocodile.

"Out of my way, or I'll snap your snouts,"
said Crocker, swimming fast.

He knocked Hugh into the air and kept
going.
"He's mean!" said Ardsley.
"And he's going to win the race," said
Hastings.

"Look out, Waldorf!" called Ardsley.
Waldorf didn't hear anything. He was
swimming as fast as he could.

Crocker got closer and closer.
I'm almost to the finish line, thought
Waldorf. Is it possible I might win?

Then Crocker bit Waldorf's tail and
yanked him back.
"Yi!" cried Waldorf.

"Stay there, you flabby fatso," said Crocker,
"and you can watch me cross the finish
line!"

"Hooray for Crocker!" cried Crocker,
wading toward the bank. "The Olympic
champ. . ."

Suddenly Crocker was hit by powerful
streams of water.

It was Hastings and Ardsley.

Crocker was knocked upside down.
Hastings and Ardsley sent him spinning
away down the river.

"All clear, Waldorf!" said Ardsley. "Looks
like you'll win the race now."
"Better hurry," said Hastings. "Hugh
is way ahead."

"Hugh worked hard for this," said Waldorf.
"I don't mind if he wins."

"Congratulations, Hugh!" called Waldorf.
"Nice going! . . .Good race!" called
    Ardsley and Hastings.

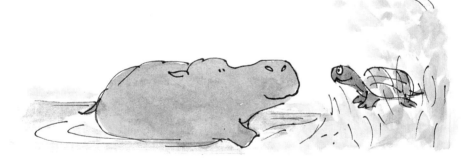

"Thanks, Waldorf," said Hugh. "I know you
    sort of let me get ahead."
"Well," said Waldorf, "Hastings and Ardsley
    sort of let *me* get ahead."

"Thanks for your help with Crocker," said
  Waldorf.
"I don't think he'll be entering the
  Olympics next year," said Hastings.
"Well, I will," said Waldorf. "Definitely."

EVENING

When the day was over, there was a picnic for everybody. There was ice cream for dessert, and then Ardsley and Hastings sang a duet.

"In my heart of hearts I wish
for more ice cream in my dish. . . ."

Mr. Crenshaw
started to tell a
story about what
the games were
like long ago . . .

but he got sleepier
and sleepier, and
before he could
finish . . .

he was
sound asleep.

Burnet and Gordon and Franklin did a
special dance called the "Skunk Shuffle."

The big surprise was when
Crocker turned up with a plate
of cookies for everybody.
"Sorry about the race today," he said
to Waldorf. "Have a cookie. I made
them myself."
"Thanks, Crocker," said Waldorf.
"Mmm . . . mind if I have another?"

Finally it was time to go home.

"Next year's games will be even better," said May.

"How could that be?" said Harold. "This year was perfect."

Soon it was quiet on the mud flat, except for Ardsley and Hastings softly singing one last song.